BATMAN BEYOND

Hear No Evil

Random House 🏠 New York
www.randomhouse.com/kids
www.dccomics.com

By Scott Peterson
Illustrated by John Delaney,
Mike DeCarlo, and David Tanguay
Batman created by Bob Kane

A Random House PICTUREBACK® Book
BATMAN and all related characters, names, and indicia are trademarks of DC Comics. Used under license. Copyright © 2002 by DC Comics.
All rights reserved under International and Pan-American Copyright Conventions. Published in the United States by Random House, Inc.,
New York, and simultaneously in Canada by Random House of Canada Limited, Toronto.
Library of Congress Control Number: 00-105893   ISBN: 0-375-80654-7
Printed in the United States of America   First Edition   May 2002 10 9 8 7 6 5 4 3 2 1
PICTUREBACK, RANDOM HOUSE, and the Random House colophon are registered trademarks of Random House, Inc.

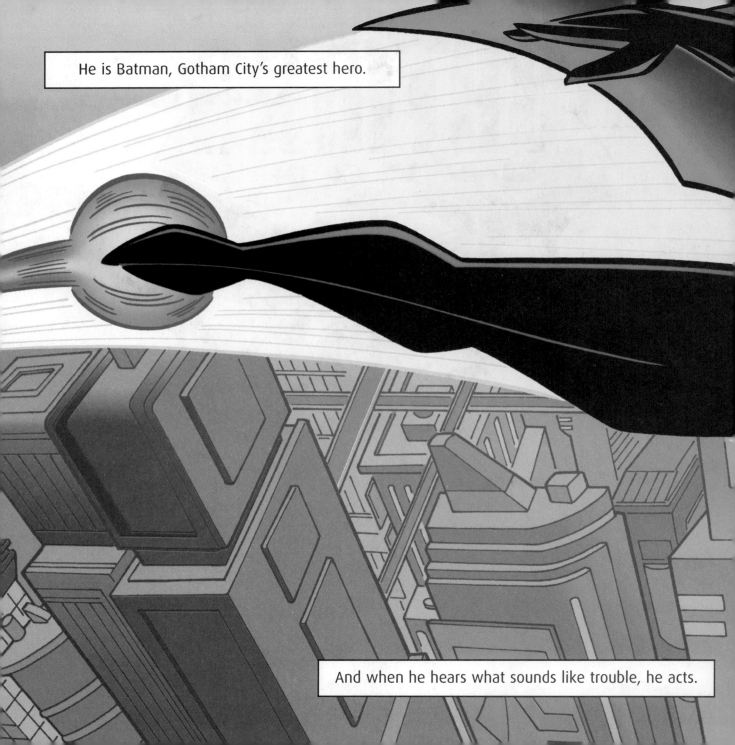